# THE PELICAN CROSSING

# THE PELICAN CROSSING

ADRIAN P CONWAY

Matador
Unit E2 Airfield Business Park,
Harrison Road, Market Harborough,
Leicestershire. LE16 7UL
Tel: 0116 2792299
Email: books@troubador.co.uk
Web: www.troubador.co.uk/matador
Twitter: @matadorbooks

ISBN 978 1803137 032

British Library Cataloguing in Publication Data.
A catalogue record for this book is available from the British Library.

Printed and bound in the UK by TJ Books Limited, Padstow, Cornwall
Typeset in 11pt Minion Pro by Troubador Publishing Ltd, Leicester, UK

Matador is an imprint of Troubador Publishing Ltd

To mum

For keeping me

*But he that hath the steerage of my course,*
*direct my sail.*

William Shakespeare

# AUTHOR BIOGRAPHY

Adrian P Conway, author of novella *The Pelican Crossing*, lives in a house near St Albans, UK with other Conways but no dog. He writes gritty, soulful, literary fiction including micro and short stories, many of which can be found on his imaginatively named *Adrian's Fiction* substack (https://adrianconway.substack.com). He is currently busy writing his first novel out of the story world of *The Pelican Crossing*. When not writing, he can be found in the kitchen and also in the kitchen at parties.

# 1

**S**hadows deepened over the autumn city as the day's last heat fled the air. Meteor felt its chill upon his cheeks but his trusty puffer, thick jeans and hoodie took care of the rest. Others weren't so savvy, undone by the rising damp, and everywhere brightly lit river bridges cleared of bustling crowds. Soon the plummeting sun was lost from view, revealing a waning moon low-set between two nearby tower blocks. All about, the streetlights of London glittered into life like substitute stars.

He slipped through the dying dusk, purposeful over home pavements. D/Cent strode beside him in good spirits, ribbing him over attempts to grow facial hair. They tussled for a time and then talked supercar spotting before nearing their destination at the extreme edge of their turf.

They came to a stop outside an end-of-terrace Pimlico townhouse. In stark contrast to the surrounding properties, it screamed absent landlords. Most of its sills were cracked or crumbling and only those with a death wish would entrust themselves to the balcony. Brickwork weeds sprouted from the facade as little instances of defiant life. He raised eyebrows at D/Cent who'd been to bash there before. D/Cent merely smirked, shrugged, and slunk in under its portico ahead of him, rucksack swinging with the weight of cans. From the top step, he noticed the heavy door had been left slightly ajar for incoming partygoers and so tracked in behind an equally cautious D/Cent.

## IIII

Meteor crossed the threshold. He clocked in D/Cent's gangly frame a familiar twitchiness as they headed up the bare-board stairs and over the landing. Their journey's end was an unexpectedly quiet flat to the left, its unnumbered door also ajar. Inside, a small nightlight provided the only illumination and the ghostly half-dark left him feeling a little uneasy. With eyes adjusting from the naked bulb of the corridor, he now noticed neatly stowed buckets and sacks as well as trip-hazard skimming floats that had been kicked all about. As they picked their way forward, their distorted silhouettes stalked the patched walls in parallel. D/Cent was grumbling about the absence of a plaster mixer which might've been worth a few Pinkies to them.

The door at the right was shut, though the low hum of voices behind it clear enough. They entered a large high-ceiling room with blacked-out windows and commandeered work-lights under blood-dark sheets, giving the place a volcanic vibe. Clumps of people stood drinking whilst local legend, DJ Retro, small torch in mouth, finished rigging up on a pasting table.

After finding a clear spot by the wall with a good view of the entrance, they cracked two of the beers they'd brought. Taking in the room and the quality of some of the newcomers, Meteor floated, 'Broh, dis party's dead, innit. Where dem gal you be promissin?' He killed the can in a oner and belched briskly in anticipation of a string of excuses.

D/Cent smirked, his signature dimples still dimly distinct. 'Wait up, Cuz. We still earlies. You see it – dem huneez be ere soon enuff.'

He instantly recognised D/Cent's *trying-to-sound-convincing* voice. 'Phh, iss on you den,' he said, 'dis place bout as dry as me brew, you git me?'

The quip had the desired effect and a chuckling D/Cent chucked him another from the bag. As he opened it, D/Cent, tapping his jacket pocket, added, 'No rush, anyhows: we got nuff blow if Lipa's a no show.'

'Sweet.' He smiled and swigged before continuing, 'So you sayin you test dis place before, den?'

'Yeh, yeh, bout six monf ago. An it were ram… an not wiv man, before you chip in… but…'

'Ohh, ere we go.'

'Nah, nah, iss juss, word gets round fo real, an next ting, ya know da flow: Boyz N Da Hood, innit. So we see, dass all me sayin.'

'Uh-huh, yeh we see ahhight.' Then his eyes settled on the entrance. 'But straight up, Broh, any signs o steel an me headin double-quick, you ear me?'

3

'Hey G, don be stressin. We be cool like Ja Rule.' Then D/Cent started singing as sweetly as a deaf donkey.

He just about recognised the song from the opening, 'Don't.'

'Yeah, iss party night…'

He sucked his teeth whilst shaking his head, 'Ladies' Night, ya tool!'

'Wait wot? Oh, yeh.'

'You forgetten bout dem huneez already, innit.' D/Cent started laughing and knuckle-knocked him. Yet, momentarily distracted like this, they missed a hooded figure, newly filling the doorframe, descending upon their position with fierce pace and purpose.

## IIII

Meteor's can slipped in his hand and beer slopped up, out and over his jeans and onto the floor. He was caught between the surprise of not having dropped it and the shoulder barge that caused it. Instinctively, he'd already squared off. From amid the adrenaline haze, came a deep voice, 'Dang niggaz, you be blind in dis ere bat cave, innit!' And with that they were gripping-up and chesting-out with MC Tru.

'Sheet Broh, we bout to go Po on yo ass!'

Meteor noted D/Cent's *trying-to-sound-convincing* voice again. 'When you get ere?' he asked.

'Juss now, innit.' Tru dropped his hood, grinning with that familiar pit-bull smile, which served to reveal the faint glint of his two gold front teeth. Meteor immediately noticed his new hairstyle set in zig-zagged cornrows just visible under a pushed-back cap.

'Ahhight Snoops, ffought you woz all too busy,' D/Cent added.

At sixteen, Tru was a couple of years older than Meteor and D/Cent but still closest to them in the crew. They'd bonded early over music, humour and partying; and also partying, and babes, and partying.

'Sort of,' he rubbed his throat, 'but s'already soo hot in ere, innit.'

'Ahhight, ahhight, if you don go spillin it all.' D/Cent handed over a can.

Although Tru's presence was unexpected, Meteor felt himself relaxing. 'Nice one. WMDs in da house!' He extended his beer and they tapped and guzzled.

Looking round, Tru enquired, 'You two d'only pussy ere, den?'

Meteor found himself snorting through foam, 'Fok Broh, you only down five secs an you bringin it!'

'Ahhight, fo real, woss da DL: tell da Tru?'

Anticipating D/Cent, Meteor mused, 'Well, Hollywood ere say dis place bout to go Vogue.' He laughed it up as Tru peered closely into D/Cent's frowning face.

'Dat riiiight?' Tru mocked.

'Hey shush up, man's twissin up man's words, innit.'

'Yeah anyhows,' Tru pulled back, 'I be earin dis ting be sweet.'

An alarm triggered in Meteor's mind. 'Where you earin dat?'

Tru shook his head casually, 'Ya kno, ere n dere.' He smiled broadly, 'Fink I come for da manchat?'

Meteor shook his head at an echoing D/Cent.

IIII

As the room gradually filled, Meteor's thoughts drifted with the smoke from a shared spliff. The music thumped away and he observed the respective mouths of D/Cent and Tru arguing over the DJ's selections. He caught the tail-end of another thread about whether *Corn$tarr* was still the UK's hottest female rapper. And now he had *that* video in his head.

A weird state of relaxed tension settled over him. Would he have felt safer with more of the crew around? Sometimes that was worse – word would get out and lead to bigger beef. Tru could handle himself, no probs – bruv was already a solid six-foot and sporty since a nipper, but string-bean D/Cent had two left feet and was no scrapper. And his prized bobbly high-top fade simply stretched out the laughs. Meteor considered himself no slouch even though somewhat short for his age. It just meant he was often underestimated to his advantage. Still, the problem these days: you never knew what was coming your way. Tasers were showing up here and there, there'd been a spate of evil acid attacks a while back and more and more man were swinging steel. A shank felt fit for *Antiques Roadshow*. Yeah, every day may be Tony Montana Day.

||||

An hour later and Meteor was grinning from ear to ear. The place pulsed as the DJ dropped a killer *back-in-the-day* signature set. Through the booming bass, a clutch of three girls came wheeling and giggling towards them. The sight spurred D/Cent and Tru to immediate action but, Meteor wasn't yet in the mood.

After a minute or so, a nonplussed D/Cent drifted back. 'Ssup, Broh?'

'Nuttin, how you gettin on?'

'Well, I kno you ent great at maff n'all, but, you can still count to t'ree, right?' D/Cent delivered the line deadpan.

Meteor, laughing inside, decided to string it out. 'Yeah, I ent feelin it, Cuz. You man enuff fo two dhough, right?'

D/Cent's brow furrowed. Meteor sensed him scrutinising his face.

'You shittin me, fo real? Dey fine, see. Dat one eyin you right now, Bruv.'

A pretty girl glanced furtively towards him. 'Nah, she ent all dat.'

D/Cent, taken aback, appeared wrapped in mental calculation, 'Wot! You waitin for da right bruva to come along?'

'Ehh, easy blud!' He scanned the room as though preoccupied, turning away to conceal his features, but it was taking all his effort not to laugh out loud.

Meteor's eyes finally came to rest on Tru. Sporting Solomon's smile, he waved as though leaving for a trip whilst somehow managing to manoeuvre his arms around all three girls. His phone lit up recording his conquest whilst a new track blew up the house.

'Come on, Cuz. Don mek me beg, innit. S'bad for da self-esteem.' D/Cent buzzed about his ear.

He smiled and, deciding to relent, said, 'Ahhight, gimme a minute to finish my beer.'

'Wot? You wafflin. Less go!' He looked towards the girls then back round, 'Noh, noh, don tell me dis is yo fantasy *Love Island* usuals? Broh, yo ent gunna meet yo wet-dream

Barbie ere or anywheres else fo dat… look, juss stand dere for tac support, innit.'

As D/Cent continued speaking, Tru returned in a self-satisfied spliff cloud, baseball cap now back to front. Meteor felt his heavy arm curl about his shoulders. 'Eyyy, dem gal wanna kno why y'all shy,' he spoke in exaggerated Jamaican patois, 'an me tell dem iss coz ya gotta dose so bad ya likkle ding-a-ling nearly fall right off,' Meteor exploded into laughter, 'an me say trusay d'only ting ya good fa grindin dese days is ya marnin caffee.' And with that, Tru had crafted the lyric of the night. After they'd recovered, he freely proffered the peace-reefer. D/Cent no longer seemed to care the girls had moved on.

||||

He was starting to feel nice. With D/Cent and Tru it never felt like a gang thing. Growing up together on their Westminster estate, you learnt the basic rule the hard way: gang or victim and not much in between – pretty much the same as whether you had some flush or were flat broke. But he'd drifted into it more than anything because, well, there wasn't much happening *Estateside* and he could only ever remember knocking about with the crew. To his mind, real gangsters were something out of *Narcos* – the ones who were really coining it – whereas this was just day by days.

||||

Curiosity saw them threading further into the flat where they discovered another smaller but less rammed room where the music wasn't quite so loud. Finding a corner, they crashed down on their puffers for props. Meteor sang along to 'Gotta Get Thru This' whilst Tru free-styled over it. No one in the crew would say it to his face (what with him being fully covered on the ego front) but Tru was easily their best rapper. He already possessed a bass voice belying his age and none of them were entirely sure where he found his words. As the crew's sole soul singer, Meteor was secure in his talent, which was backed up by a pitch-perfect memory for tunes. He and Tru had already produced and recorded some of their own tracks in a council studio facility, well, before it closed due to lack of funding. Thankfully, D/Cent sat nodding in silence, partly because he was their mixologist and partly because they'd just shouted at him again to stop making their ears bleed with his braying.

And maybe that was what bound them together most: shared hope of commercial success – code for *gettin outta Dodge!* It can happen, but it seemed the route from A to C was always through B, and that B was *business*. It was never about steaming gullible kids for phones and cash or even fucking them up for the sake of it. That was more Muzz-L's style. No, more like maintaining reliable revenues and knowing man's got your back. Which on the street can make all the difference.

Take Charlton – D/Cent's cousin. It always made Meteor smile that they'd named the nipper after their footie team. And that was just it: turned out to have mad skills. Destiny or what? They lived somewhere over Woolwich way and, as D/Cent tells it, he'd just made the youth squad so everyone was completely made up. He wasn't really in a gang but the whole school and hood knew him, including local Gs. And to rivals – in this case *Shooters Hill Steel* – that made him fair game. No back-up, see. Meteor still felt sick in his stomach for D/Cent's family.

They'd had their own scrapes too. He ran a finger over a horizontal scar a little too close to the underside of his left eye, which was a scratch compared to the one on his lower right arm, concealed as much as possible. Yeah, he may've been short but was fast and hit hard when necessary. Turf is turf. What can you do? To paraphrase the Big Guy: *man can't live on B alone.* No, but you'll never get to C if there's nothing left of your daily B.

# 2

'**B**woy who dat gal?' Meteor was on his feet.

'Where?' D/Cent, who for some reason was wearing shades, slipped them down his nose before replying.

'Singin over dere.'

'Don kno it, Cuz… Tru?' Tru shook his head.

'Now *she* be sweet.'

'Well, she may be sweet but she also wiv dat big bruva by da looks of it,' Tru chipped in before slumping back down.

Meteor continued observing her closely, mindful of Tru's words. 'Nah, reckon dey juss hangin togevva, innit.'

D/Cent stood up next to him. 'You seen im before?'

'Nah…' he swigged from his can, 'but he don look all dat.'

D/Cent and Tru erupted into laughter.

'Ahhight, easy Joshua!' Tru said.

He chose to ignore them, 'She dress sweet too, you kno.'

D/Cent's fist connected with the dead spot on his arm, 'Wot *now* you ready, Dred Ken!'

He rubbed it whilst continuing, 'Phhh, she got some shape.'

'Ey Tru, wot you reckon his chances?'

Meteor turned to hear a deep voice from the middle of a smoke cloud, 'Pussseeeeyyyyyy.'

He looked at D/Cent with raised eyebrows who just shrugged. Returning his eyes to the prize he said, 'I gotta see if she'll check me.'

'Cuz, you wrecked as Tru, innit.' He heard D/Cent's words following after him. 'See you in ten, den,' and then much louder, 'seconds dat is!'

## ||||

For a good three or four tracks, he hovered behind the group in a position calculated to catch the girl's eye. Her girlfriend seemed to notice him first, with enough whispering and smiling between them to offer a ray of hope. Except Goliath kept cutting off his view in calculated steps. Feeling the need for some Dutch courage, he returned to grab another beer.

'Not sure we got one cold enuff, you git me?' D/Cent jibed.

Whilst Meteor smirked and guzzled, Tru treated them to his latest thoughts:

> 'Come priddy lady an lehs get jiggy
> Leh me introduce ya to mah not-so-biggy

Meteor's mah name, like da shootin star
A light to ya life an a hand in ya bra

Me sing super-sweet like da nightingale
Soul-serenader of da fines tail
Fill up ya dreams wid eternal summer.'

He paused to cough, clearly pleased with its effect, before applying the finishing touch:

'Yeah, fanks for da pox, babes – sumtin of a bummer'

The joke had history. D/Cent bounced about whooping it up in front of him. Still smirking, he shook his head and left them to it.

## IIII

By the time he returned she was nowhere to be seen. *Goliath's doing, no doubt!* He felt his heart sink as he scanned the room which now seemed twice as full as before. A body-heat haze choked the air as he pushed his way through thickets of revellers. His hoodie began to cling uncomfortably and stinging sweat fogged his vision. He became acutely conscious of knocking into people's drinks: whole places had kicked off for less. Eventually, reaching the opposite wall, he found a little space and some cooler air. It wasn't looking good.

After finishing his beer and removing his hoodie, he felt a little less clammy and ready for another reccy. Standing on tip-toes, he caught a glimpse of what might've been her bright sunflower top, in the kitchen area. As he edged round the wall, the DJ dropped the 'Just in Case' remix and the whole place erupted. There was nothing for it but to keep his head down and bounce along with the crowd, pushing as best he could where openings presented.

The plan was to regain eye-contact, give *Goliath* the slip, and make his move from there. Halfway across the floor, though, the crowd became too dense so he turned back for the wall. And, after squeezing past two or three dancers, found himself standing, sweetly surprised, right behind her. His eyes traced the arch of her bare back from the halter downwards. A ponytail danced playfully about her shimmering skin but failed to distract his attention away from her sweet ass. She turned abruptly as though having been touched, her face a dead ringer for a back-in-the-day Brandy, except for the slim, rectangular glasses set cute upon her mid-nose. His spontaneous smile immediately mirrored in hers and, with great relief, the distance between them simply melted away.

## IIII

Meteor was in a million happy places. Her perfect hips, swinging with the rhythm, swept the room before them, whilst their bodies pulsed together like stars in endless night. When it came, that first kiss was pure killer. Her mouth felt soft and slick like warm butter and her plump lips tasted faintly of Parma Violets. And magic. His ears still burned from the touch of her fingers, as though licked by candle flame.

She whispered something but the adjacent bass speaker obliterated all attempts to chat so she pointed to a quieter corner and led him by the hand when he nodded. He had the rear-view pleasure once more, and she turned her head to return smile for smile when the DJ dropped 'A Little Bit of Luck'. It was already feeling a lot more than that.

It had only just occurred to him that he hadn't yet devised any burns for D/Cent and Tru when a heavy bulk slammed into him from behind, instantly breaking their joined hands and sending his body sideways.

## IIII

The arms clamping his frame lifted his feet clean off the floor. He had a split second to register the fear on her face before being smashed into dancers this way and that. The panic gripping him finally fuelled a response when he saw the nearest sash window looming. It was only a familiar growl near his ear that halted him. Tru was a joker but, even so, this was way off a laugh. Craning about, he clocked the panicked look etched on D/Cent's face and realised it was serious.

Tapping Tru's flank for release, Meteor then hot-footed it with them. He lifted the lock, D/Cent yanked up the frame and within seconds they were all on the building's balcony. After checking the coast was clear at street level, they momentarily hung down like disoriented bats before hitting the ground. Tru handed him his jacket and with that they were away. At the nearest corner, Meteor slowed to look back, concrete setting thick in the centre of his chest.

'Sorry, Cuz, business-business,' Tru said halting, still blowing a little.

'Who?' he asked, eyes fixed hard.

'KLs!' D/Cent interjected. 'Ten, maybe more,' he added, 'lucky I spot dem movin in in time.'

He nodded emptily.

'Fok,' Tru flexed out his shoulders, 'Close call, innit.'

Meteor brooded on his loss as they strolled toward safer streets; not giving a crap about *Knife-Life* or any other rival gang for that matter.

## ||||

With Tru deliberately knocking into him, his focus snapped back to the present.

'Cheshire Cat get da cream, den?'

He tried not to respond.

'So woss er name, ey?' D/Cent invaded his face space.

'I forgit,' he replied, smirking. Tru gave him a playful dig in the ribs. 'Ahhight, Jaycee, innit. All I got, bruv.'

'Wot, no digits! Don be shittin me.'

He stopped to beam at them both, 'You kno, wiv all da commotion, I fink I mussave forgot em.'

'My G, Meteor, da comedian!' Tru stated. And after a moment's pause, they were all in stitches.

# 3

Over an hour later, another group trudged the streets in the opposite direction, the freezing air far warmer than the mood. In a thin, tiny cardigan, a distracted and shivering Jaycee wandered along link-armed with her friend Suren. *Goliath* strutted beside them listening to music through wireless headphones. Jaycee stopped short, her features downcast. Under the light-fall of a nearby lamppost, she shook her head at *Goliath* who raised his eyebrows and shrugged.

'I juss can't believe it,' she said heavily.

'Sorry,' he stated, sounding not. Suren shaded him. 'Wot?' He shifted away a little. ''S true.'

'He woz sooo cute, dough.' Her head dropped again.

'Maybe ee's goddit wrong, Sis,' Suren gripped her arm.

'I ent,' *Goliath* intoned flatly. 'You reckon iss a party piece to leave by da window?'

He was all the comfort of cold coffee, but Jaycee knew the truth of it. The boy named Meteor was WMD. It mattered little she'd no gang affiliations. She lived in a different postcode; different turf. In other words, another world. Her's belonged to Wolfpak. WMDs owned the other. Darnell headed them, A:pex ran Wolfpak, and they were increasingly in dispute over territory. *Goliath* said he even recognised some of the latecomers as Battersea *Knife-Life* – bad news they felt bold enough to cross the bridge at night. It was all too much. Everyone knew the unspoken rule: gang or not, no crossing lines. Except, lines had been crossed.

## IIII

In the unyielding cold, Jaycee slipped into silence and Suren curled an arm about her shoulders.

'Thass just my luck, you kno.' She felt something more than disappointment.

'Maybe best forgit about it… you kno, da whole night.'

Jaycee stared at her blankly.

'Plenny more fish, right?' As she spoke, Suren's nose stud winked with lamp light. 'Better find out now than later, ey?'

The words numbed more than the air.

'Ey,' Suren stopped her, 'you kno I'm right, right?'

'I guess.' She felt suddenly unclean.

'You might wanna block iss number… if you goddit,' *Goliath* fished.

'Juss shut it, Marcus.' His smirky manner had irked her once more.

He sucked his teeth as they pushed on.

'Wot if I kepp it quiet?' They were more dribbled thoughts than intended words. Marcus's gaze swung towards her, matched by Suren's meeting his.

'You kno dass not a good idea, Sis. Save yoself da pain.'

'But, you wouldn say nuffin, would you?'

'Sis, wot you sayin? I got you, but dis ent goin nowhere. You gotta be real.'

'I kno, I kno… but.'

'No buts. You kno how it plays… if *she* gets wind.'

She winced a reply.

**A** nother cutting winter's night on the block saw the three of them fuming breath into cupped hands. They were hanging under the arches near Tru's crib, their preferred haunt when away from the full crew. Snapz, another WMD, had just split due to the cold and Meteor was about to do the same when Tru, casually kicking a concrete strut, enquired:

'So you bin seein dis gal or wot?'

'Well, you kno.' Meteor felt himself blush upon hearing his unconvincing response.

'Nooo, I don kno, fam, dass why I askin, innit!' It was Tru's teasing tone.

He smirked, shrugging evasively.

D/Cent swung in by Tru's side, knocking his arm to egg him on. 'So, you got ta firss base, den?'

There was no way he was going to open up. Tru was too good a piss-taker even if it was safe to talk.

'Ahhight Dark Knight, keep yo secrets, den.' After a pause, Tru tried a different tack. 'Is she fine? She look fine.'

He held out, despite D/Cent's snorting.

'Yeahh, dat sweet ass.' Tru started making hip-circles, mimicking Meteor's dancing.

He felt himself cracking.

'She a good grind?'

Finally, he relented, taking a mock swing at Tru. Even as he did, he felt the phone vibrating in his pocket. Message for message.

## IIII

Jaycee tried to resist his contact during that first week, but her will to do so quickly faded. He was funny, and persistent in the right way. Initially, she felt flattered but a deepening desire set in that took her a little by surprise. The photo messaging had certainly spiced up in the second week. As she stretched on her bed, sinking into the pillows and staring up at nothing in particular, her arms moved to cradle her favourite Jellycat. Against all sense and with each waking one, she longed to return to those lips that felt they were meant for hers alone.

# 5

ithin D/Cent's familiar giraffey flounce, Meteor detected something odd as the distance closed between them. Immediately after knuckling up, D/Cent began swinging his head from side to side, as though rehearsing silent lines. Meteor furrowed his brow but D/Cent, avoiding eye-contact, missed it. So he began mimicking his movements which eventually had the desired effect.

'Eyy, listen cuz, I be talkin to Tru earlier, innit.' It was D/Cent's trying-to-sound-casual voice.

'Oh yeah, woss man wafflin bout now?'

'Nah, nah, ent like dat… he ahh… sed to speak to ya… you kno, direc like.'

'Bout wot?'

There was a pause.

'Yo gal.' The words came out flat and humourless. He'd still barely looked up.

'Wot bout er?' Meteor consciously hardened his tone.

The reply came as though poorly rehearsed: 'Sooo, Tru be sayin dat, you kno, he clocked er, like… earlier today,' D/ Cent finally raised his eyes, 'up Vic Place, innit.'

As the content didn't yet tally with the tone, Meteor pushed past D/Cent's loaded looks. 'Ahhight?'

'An, well, so…' He shifted uneasily again.

'Juss spit it, broh.'

'She be mixin wiv dem Wolfpak.' The words rushed out, each landing like a brick.

He stared wide-eyed at D/Cent who, in the end, had to look away.

'Straight?'

D/Cent nodded.

As the heavy high-road traffic pushed past in thunderous disregard, he wrestled with what he'd heard.

'You kno dere's no messin wiv dis sorta ting, bruv… wiv all da beef, innit.'

He could feel a minute twitching in his upper right eyelid, which often set in with tiredness. And D/Cent's stating of the bleedin obvious had hardly made his own response immediately obvious. His chest tightened as he began to speak: 'Tell me how Tru say it. Precise, ahhight.'

'So dat she were wiv dem, chattin n style.' He must have read Meteor's mind because he quickly continued, 'Right, but, fo real, he didn say dat she woz actin like crew.'

Meteor nodded, but then, spurred by D/Cent's narrowing eyes, stated as breezily as possible: 'K, me check it out. Ahhight, laterz.' He held out a fist before turning to go.

'Fo sho.' D/Cent seemed caught between thoughts.

He shouted back, 'An reespex to Tru, yeh,' before pacing away into the dark.

# 6

eading the message he instantly knew it was a great idea. They'd been struggling to find somewhere safe that was far enough away yet still within easy reach. Especially with all the recent escalations. In his whole life such a place had never crossed his mind, which is why it was perfect.

Even as he pushed through the winter storm, he still couldn't quite believe entry was free. Once across the busy road, the white stone building stretched upwards proudly, like some rich man's mansion. He felt uncomfortable scaling the steps towards the entrance, the huge columns hanging by the door like bouncers. Then again, he figured that was the point. He quickly passed under the words etched TATE BRITAIN and, with relief, spied Jaycee waiting for him just inside.

Despite his soaked puffer, she hurried over to hug him tight and the world instantly righted. They wandered off into various galleries but what else was going to hold his attention? She was prettier every time. Still, when they reached what looked like the main room, he remembered what needed addressing. Guiding her towards a free bench in the middle, he tried to copy D/Cent's trying-to-sound-casual voice.

'You bin spyin on me, Meteor?' She looked askance whilst smiling.

'Nahh, man sez he saw you is all, you kno, by chance, innit.' Whispering made it hard to find the right tone.

She searched his face. 'Yeah, I kno some o dem from school, but I ent crew if dass wot you finkin.'

'Nah, nah, babes, but… wot, do dey kno bout me?'

'What! You crazy, babes? You on da full down-low – apart from my girlfriend from da party an she ent no crewsta eivver.'

He searched her face.

'Hey, wot you stressin over?' She lifted one of his hands to place it within hers, kissing the palm tenderly. When she returned his gaze her eyes were wide and inviting.

He softened a little, 'Nuttin, nuttin, but…'

'Hmm?' She ran a hand over his head and, cupping the back of his scalp, pulled him in for a lingering kiss.

When they broke, Meteor continued, 'Iss juss, you kno,' but before he could finish, she'd once more set a seal upon his lips. His hands sought her waist, one coming to rest on the rise of her rear. He could feel a tightening. She reset her glasses when they unlocked and Meteor tried to recall his last physics class.

As he stared ahead, the painting directly in front caught

his eye. After a moment, he stood up and they walked over to it hand in hand. Some crazy-looking white lady lay face-up in a river, all covered in pretty, bright flowers. Reading the sign, he sounded out her strange name in his head a few times. Though her dress was sort of sexy, the eyes were steely and distant. It was weird. She had decent breasts and her mouth was parted slightly as though inviting a kiss but, well, it also looked a little like her last breath. She was just a painting, a world away, yet he found himself feeling strangely sorry for her.

Her soft voice sounded in his ear, 'Listen babes, I know enuff about Wolfpak not to say nuffing in front of dem, you know, especially A:pex. She not right in da head dat gal.'

Meteor felt an increasing sense of relief as he turned towards her, 'Ahhight, but you kno da way tings are goin, dere's gonna be hell to pay sooner dan later.'

'Everyone knos she be tryna spread her ends but dey don't talk business outside da crew an I kno enuff to keep my mouf shut tight about you, is all.' She raised her eyebrows. 'Hmm?' He felt her hands gripping his hips as they pressed into one another again. After a moment, he pulled out a touch.

'You sooo sweet, you kno?'

'Yeah, I kno it.' She fluttered her lashes affectedly and tilted her head slightly. 'But only for you.'

He laughed at first but then his thoughts ran on. 'But wot me sayin is: now we bowf kno dis, we be runnin mad risks carryin on, an, you kno…' But her mouth stole away the rest of his words.

Slowly they made their way together out of the main gallery, heading towards the cafe, but not before Meteor took a final glance at the sad, pale girl staring into that endless sky.

# 7

By more than the mere thrill of illicit things, by more than even the crippling fear of repercussions, Meteor was driven on; a golden ache now accompanying his every breath.

It struck him that he'd never waited so long before *getting down to business*. It'd been over a month which was unheard of. Not that he hadn't wanted to, obviously, but circumstances had thwarted them. Then again, she was special so it needed to feel right. Anyway, that time had passed because the coming Saturday was *the* day. Her mum would be going away for the weekend so they'd have the flat to themselves. He could think of nothing else.

||||

They got lucky, managing to grab one of the few sofas in the gallery café just as the previous couple were leaving. For a time it was bathed in soft sunlight and he sat, hands interlocked with hers, enjoying spring's first blaze. The garden's patio doors were flung wide open to the season, like a hopeful preacher's arms, whilst safely beyond a huge laurel hedge the world raged on without them.

They'd been together for well over three months now. Somehow they'd made it work, despite everything. He felt they'd done all they could and, in any case, there was no going back. Whatever came next, it couldn't be measured against this. This was real. Crazy, but real. Without planning, everything else had fallen in behind it. Yeah, there was the day to day but now also this wilder thing. There's always a way. His mum taught him this. You may have to fight for it, but you'll get there if your heart is true.

She broke his train of thought: 'Yeh, the actin's going real well.'

'Yeh? You gonna be a film star, eh?'

'Don joke… iss mad competitive, dough.'

'Ey, who can resist dis smile?'

She giggled. 'But, you kno, if it don work out then it can always lead to ovva fings, like singin n dancin… but, I like actin best.'

'Wot is dis fo, like da school play or summin?'

'Nah, dere's dis projec at da community centre twice a week. All da professional courses are bucks, you kno. But, mebbe one day I can get some sponsorship.'

'Fo real, I sponsor you… an when we's superstars in LA you can pay me back.'

She laughed again. 'I fought I woz already a star?'

He smiled. Cute. 'Dang right, babes.'

They kissed lightly and then once more with deeper desire.

# 8

E ven reckoning with the smog, a clear day in late spring is
something special in the capital. A sweet heat filled the
air, wiping away all memories of the long, grimy winter.
The flood of a million blooms reached their happy nostrils
as they mooched along the path around St James's Park lake.
He'd decided it was far enough away from usual territories to
risk being outdoors.

A copper-coloured cockapoo, covered with twigs and
leaves, scampered out from beneath a nearby bush, causing
them to laugh. Crouching down, Jaycee called to it and he
watched her with pleasure as she tickled its belly. It soon
bolted, though, following its owner's call. As they walked on
together, he told her about a new tune he'd written just for

her – 'She's Off Da Hook' – and started singing it. When she said she loved it, he was so happy he strutted about imitating a peacock in its prime. Then, when she curled her index finger at him, he pretended to be the dog returning, making her laugh all the more.

Holding her tight under the dappled light of a London Plane tree, his mum's voice returned unexpectedly: *the good Lord don't ever take back His graces, son, but you can let them slip through your fingers.* The sudden strangeness of the words at that moment lifted him out of himself to look upon the park as though for the first time. Familiarity instantly stole back in but for a split second it was as though the whole world had fallen silent. He noticed that Jaycee had turned to veil her face and that goosebumps now covered her arms. He was just about to ask her if everything was alright when she bellowed:

'Wot da fuck is dat duck?!'

He followed her gaze: 'You serious, babes?'

'Yeh, I'm serious.'

'Yo, dass a pelican, innit.'

'Iss massive.'

'Fo real, dey mad you kno: eat da park pigeon straight down, innit.'

'Nooo way, dey don!'

'I swear, live n whole. You see em trapped inside da gullet, flappin about, tryna escape.'

'Ohh, dass gross.' She placed a hand over her mouth.

The bird, the size of a small child, squatted on a bench in the sunlight. As they watched, it unfurled its extraordinary wings to their fullest extent and shook them out. There was no mistaking: this was its domain and right here it was top of the food chain.

The weirdness of the previous moment seemed to pass and they strolled on. He was content to enjoy her chatter. In fact, he'd never known her so vocal. It gave him time to…

'Meteor, are you lissnin?'

'Wot? Yeh, yeh. I juss enjoyin da sun, innit.'

'Why you lookin at me like dat?'

'Phhh, you so sweet, you know.'

'Yeh, you ent so bad eivva.'

She swung her body into him, kissing him almost too hard on the mouth. The press of her soft breasts set his loins alight, gripping him with a familiar longing. When he leant out to make a suggestion, he noticed a flicker of sadness pass across her face, as brief as the breeze upon the lake. She made to shake it off but this time he knew what he'd seen and, putting two and two together, asked: 'You ahhight?'

'Yeh, yeh.' She sighed deeply.

'Listen, if da pressure's gettin too much, babes.'

She placed a hand on his cheek as the tears tumbled down her own. It was as though scales had fallen from his eyes, to see the toll everything was taking on her.

'Hey, hey,' he tried to thumb away the tears, 'if you need some space… you kno, to cool tings for a time… take da weight off.' He hated every single word.

She continued to cry quietly, holding onto him. Eventually, she replied: 'Iss juss, da longer we go, da more likely one day we get seen… in da end. Right?'

His mind jammed with competing versions of reality. 'But we longways outta sight ere, babes. We juss keep it clever, like we bin doin.' He was about to add *and something will work itself out* but he didn't like the sound of it even to himself.

She looked away across the sunlit park, her face sparkling and sad. He rocked her body to and fro, trying to transfer some fighting spirit. 'We can stick to da Tate for a bit, if you worried.' To his relief she smiled a little and then perked up over the rest of the afternoon. He was greatly relieved, not least because they had the flat to themselves again. Having then bought them each a 99 with two flakes, nuts and strawberry sauce, they threaded their way through to Green Park and sat on the grass enjoying them as the sun slowly slipped from the sky.

# ||||

That night, her body brimmed. She felt ripe and taut, almost swollen. Maybe the flat's thermostat was set too high but they were very soon sweaty and breathless. She put it down to being on the pill but he felt something else, less certain.

He was groggy when woken later for more. The clock display was dimmed and she didn't reply when asked the time. Soon he didn't care. Tiredness escaped him like a flock of startled birds as she bore down on him with the same unsettling urgency. The room was dark and dense with desire and she came hard even though he had a way to go. In the pause, she kissed him persistently, smiled, and then started up again as though desperately needing his help to reach somewhere lost inside.

# 9

At least for a while, Jaycee seemed happier sticking to the gallery. The last couple of weeks, though... he was at a bit of a loss.

Having met inside the foyer, he suggested they get out. A beautiful summer's day held some prospect of lifting her mood, despite her resistance. If they stuck to the river path, heading away from Millbank towards the Houses of Parliament, they'd be safe enough.

Passing in and out of the ever-shifting shade of the plane trees, they distracted themselves with the many boats tearing up and down the Thames. Jaycee remained quiet, hardly responding to his attempts at chit-chat. Nearing Lambeth Bridge, it dawned on him that she hadn't even properly smiled the whole time. *What the hell? Had it been a bad idea to go out?* A new, most unwelcome thought wormed its way into his mind.

'Jaycee?'

'Don't.'

'Wot? I ent even sed nuffin yet.'

'Don't look at me dat way.'

'Wot way?' She was starting to vex him a little. 'Woss goin on?' He paused a moment before the words forced their way out. 'You tryna kill dis, innit?'

She somehow lost her footing on the flat floor. He caught her from falling hard but she still ended up on all fours. Her shoulders were shaking, which at first he took for laughter but, once crouched down, quickly realised his mistake. Drawing her to him, her rag doll form collapsed over him with heavy sobbing. Next to a nearby kids' playground he spied a bench and so, after a time, gently raised and walked her to it, burying his embarrassment before the rubbernecking mums as he sat silently holding her hand.

## IIII

'Look, I geddit, babes. If you can' do dis no more.' He rubbed the back of her hand softly. 'I kno iss fokked. Always hidin, always wondrin. But, I wouldn let nuffin happen to you, you kno dat.' His words failed to lift the sadness and she remained dumbstruck so he simply continued cradling her frame.

After a time, he clocked a cafe shack beyond the merry-go-round. 'Hey, I get some water, ahhight?' Her head nodded against him.

Tears greeted his return. He felt like crap, clearly having misjudged the burden. Eventually, barely audible over the city noise, her flat voice stated: 'I can' do it, Meteor. I can' go on.'

He had to look away from her bloodshot eyes. As he shook his head, she slipped his grasp to blow her nose into a tissue. What was there to say? To fix this? Anger burned furnace-bright within. He sprung up and paced about, still shaking his head. As he did, laughter from other people's lives spilled over the river wall, having escaped the decks of passing pleasure boats.

## IIII

She called to him and he was there in a flash.

'I'm so scared, Meteor, an I don kno wot to do.'

He sat with her again but didn't have the words so kept quiet. After a while she started shifting about, as though building to break the overstretched silence. He considered whether, for her sake, it was time to face the music. Maybe they had ridden their luck. But, what, part ways? Even if for the best, he no longer had a clue how to let go. And saying any of this wasn't going to help. As he looked upon her, she appeared, even in sorrow and tears, more beautiful than he could ever remember.

'Dere's no escape is dere, Meteor?'

Holding her as tight as he could, there at the edge of the children's playground, he thought of his mum and all her wonderful words, and quickly wiped a tear from his own eye before she noticed.

# 10

Tru by name and nature. Tough love, I guess. Mincing your mates but not your words. Says it's long past putting an end to it. And ain't any easier said as done. Keeps on about keeping it real. That facts are facts. Wolfpak jacking up the attacks; Darnell on the war-path. Reality. You know, *whilst I've been distracted.* Tells me the latest: a WMD hopper with his face fucked up from a supply sting. Anything even vaguely smelling of Wolfpak is betrayal. End of.

In a different setting, says he understands, brother-to-brother, how hard it'll be. Knows a thing or two. A name I've never heard before. Much as I'm ever gonna get. But what must be, must be. Like some corny rap. But not.

Recalling later, Meteor could still feel the spot where Tru

gripped his arm. As he rubbed it, he heard again those two parting words: *End it, bruv!*

## IIII

On a Saturday when they would've been together, he sat alone in the main gallery in their spot. He'd stood creepily close until the chump occupying it before him felt compelled enough to leave. The place had a way of making him feel less alone. Not much, but enough. And at least it was away from all the other crap.

He stared at the woman in the water. Moving on didn't seem to suit her either. Drawing close again, he noticed she was blushing. *Huh, maybe not so cold then.* Still, it was hard to tell what was on her mind. Her hands were raised skyward, reminding him of the swaying ladies at church. Was it prayer and praise, though? It might even be despair. And up close her mouth looked a lot less sexy. Yeah, she was sad alright. He knew enough about that now. Then it came to him. How could he not have noticed? The water. Like all those baptisms. Well, maybe. Ophelia wasn't a Christian name he'd ever heard of and she didn't exactly look happy being born again. Whatever her woes, though, she was at least safe inside her fancy picture frame.

As he stepped back, his mind turned to Jaycee and the brutal punishments that would've been dished out – if they'd been caught. He gagged slightly at the thought he'd put her in harm's way. Had he just been selfish, to ever think they had a chance? Like Tru said. Yeah, but Tru's eyes weren't half as sure as his words. And his own words to Jaycee had been half-baked: *cooling off, laying low, biding time* – and even these hadn't been easy to say. But in the end they had been said and, in truth, it was way too risky to hook up. The way it ended hadn't been neat, but he knew he'd never have been able to say those other words.

The flowers in the painting now reminded him of the park. He breathed out Jaycee's name, trying to push away the pain. The painted lady remained unmoved before him. Even the flowing stream was still. Fixed forever. Yeah. A man force-coughed close by, bringing him back to himself. He may've spoken her name aloud. A new chill clung to the air. Or perhaps he'd just lingered too long. He nodded towards her with increased respect, doubtful he'd ever return.

# 11

It was like she knew. They say that, don't they? When two people get close. She'd stopped responding to his messages over two weeks ago. He should've stopped, he knew that. He did at number twenty or so. Seems like she'd adjusted better, that's all. How many ways can you say *we gotta talk, babes* when you both know *we gotta not*? Although he didn't like the idea of her making the final call, it had taken the pressure off. One sort, anyway.

Ditching his number would be a watershed. Tru *strongly* suggested it but he'd been stalling for days. Resignation was just setting in when a new message pinged for his attention. He was in the local newsagents buying some sweets when, lifting his phone, there it was before him:

> hey birthday boy, saturday, park, usual
> time? miss you so much JC xxx

Wow! It had been well over a month. He ran over the words. She'd remembered. Either way, it wasn't a good idea. At all. *Miss you so much.* Dang! He was actually sweating. In a moment of blind resolve, he was about to delete it when another message toppled in on top:

> can't be without you...

Fok! Jab-jab-jab-hook. Stepping out of the shop he popped the lolly out of his mouth and called her number. It bounced to voicemail: '*Hi, this is Jaycee, if you know me leave a message.*' He hung up and immediately tried again. Same. *Hmmm.*

Look, he could be cautious. Knew the moves. Maybe. For this once. Special occasion. One last time.

# 12

Twenty minutes before the eleven o'clock meet, Meteor entered the shimmering park. Memories of good times filled his mind triggered by the rich summer fragrances flooding his senses. Tourists in masses milled about here and there, putting him immediately at ease: less chance of funny business. Sight-lines were sharp too; he'd spot any trouble a long way off. It's why he felt happy with the venue. Familiarity reduces risk. Tru would've stopped him coming, for sure. D/Cent? Meteor felt he would have backed him. Either way, he needed to give Jaycee a chance to… well, more honestly give himself the opportunity to… end it properly.

A crowd was in the way, gathered round the perfect

pelican. As he threaded past, it extended its bright wings to the full. The power of the flashback stopped him in his tracks. As he looked on, the last of the morning's pond mist split the sun's rays about the bird, encircling it in a spray of light. It was truly a sight to see! Like everyone else, he reached for his phone and took a few snaps. Whilst it was out, he checked for messages then looked up and about. No Jaycee. Yet. He was still a little early. The damp weed funk of the water reached his nostrils upon a slight breeze and he wondered if it wasn't partly the reek of digested pigeon.

||||

Having completed a full circuit of the lake, he was back by the little cottage garden with its patchwork of blooming flowers. By now it was quarter past. Five more minutes and he'd call it a day. What had been the point of it all? As he searched his suspicions, a prickly sensation on the back of his neck caused him to lift up his eyes. Heading in from a long way off, on the path near Horse Guards Parade, he saw her. On her own. She hadn't yet set eyes on him.

Keeping his peripheral vision keen, he walked with purpose to meet her.

||||

At a few metres apart they both stopped, facing one another. Her oversized sunnies totally obscured her eyes. Now that the moment was upon him, he realised he hadn't a clue what he was supposed to be feeling. Apart from maybe confusion. She looked different – smaller somehow. It was really weird.

That's when he noticed the tears leaking from under her shades. Then he knew what to do.

As he clasped her in his arms and kissed her tenderly upon the cheek, he felt cracked open like the earth's crust, and shuddered before the abyss. Her hot breath singed his ear, words trickling in like lava: 'You need to know that I love you, Meteor.' Whatever he'd expected from their forbidden date, this wasn't it. Fearing he was going to throw up, he had to step back a sec to catch his breath. She wouldn't let go of his hands so he took in deep draughts of air where he stood, in the wordless space that had them surrounded.

As he slowly recovered, she pulled him gently towards her and he sank his face into the fragrance of her hair. His own tears released into the soft strands as she gripped him tight. He lifted her sunglasses and cradled her face before they kissed urgently. There was nothing to consider and nothing left to say. In a world short on answers they'd found at least one beyond question. And it was worlds away from being the least.

# 13

The last spark of sunlight kissed the distant horizon presaging the coming of night, but it would be warm well into the evening. They sat on the grass eating burgers. Whilst admiring his birthday present, Meteor's mind raced in and out of one dead end after another. They'd both agreed they couldn't be apart and then just stared at each other knowing it counted for nothing. He felt twitchy, and tight with the food. Lying back on the grass he gazed upwards whilst Jaycee checked her messages again. She said her mum was always stressing these days. He shook his head: hardly a star to be seen. Seriously, how many out there silently crossing the city yet totally lost from view? Maybe it was too early.

He sat up and she quickly pocketed her phone. She smiled and nodded when he asked if her mum was OK. In the mellow half-light of the departing sun, her face had softened to a burnished bronze and his heart skipped a beat. Yet even as he looked on, hope stuck in his chest like the fries in his guts. The whole thing was a trap from start to finish. *Don't.* The word the world only ever seemed to offer them. Yeah, he knew they had to end what couldn't be ended before it was ended for them, but what help was knowing? She started sobbing again and he wrapped a consoling arm around her shoulders as best he could. Promise felt all out of promise.

'You could come back.'

He didn't immediately recognise her voice. 'Wot? Wow! No. I mean, you kno, course I'd love to, but...' Crossing territories would be crazy in the circumstances. She looked away. 'I ent rejectin you, babes. I juss, you kno how it be.' She turned to hold his gaze. He struggled to read her normally expressive eyes through the creeping mask of dusk.

'I really need you to, you kno...' And with that she was up.

The words had an odd flatness to them and her smile read like regret. He didn't want her pity but already his spirit leapt like a deer. Magma spewed from new fissures within and he began pacing nervously. His heart pounded inside his ears like the call of an ancient drum. Seeking calm and sense, he took deeper breaths. A breeze of cotton-wool cool swirled about his skull bringing a little relief. Another breath. Then another. It carried the scents of a city smaller and more pathetic than he'd ever known.

Her hands were held out to him in something like supplication whilst the tears kept streaming. *What the hell*!

Time was already up if grief was all they had to offer each other. Or maybe it was time to push back. As he stood, his mouth just erupted with the pressure:

'I ent comin,' he choked, 'before iss sed straight too. You da one, Jaycee. Dass it, right dere. Iss only you, nuffin but you.' He felt the tears scalding his cheeks.

'Oh my God! Oh my God!' She covered her mouth with her hands and crashed down onto her knees. It looked like she couldn't breathe, causing him to panic. Taking off his t-shirt, he waved it frantically in front of her until she seemed to calm. As she was recovering, he noticed her looking round this way and that, like some twitchy pigeon. Once re-clothed, he tried to raise her. To his surprise she felt feather light and they found themselves, after a near stumble, finally standing face-to-face. She looked drained and Meteor knew the evening was dead – even with the best will in the world. He was about to ask if she felt any better when he heard the following:

'Meteor, we could run away right now.'

'Wot. You kiddin again. Where we go?'

'I don care, anywhere. Less juss go. Now. To da flat. I pack some stuff, then we get some of yours and…' the hyperventilating started once more.

'Calm it, babes, please.' He placed a hand on her arm. 'You really stressin me.'

'We need to go. Less go.'

'Why you rush rush all of a sudden?' He nearly started laughing.

She composed herself. He waited for her to speak but she'd closed her eyes and was deep breathing again. When she opened them, her gaze seemed to pass right through him.

He shook his head. 'Wot? Wassup?'

# 14

'Meteor, I'm so sorry.'

It'd already proven a long evening. 'Look, I've told you it ent yo fault, babes. You gettin worked up fo nuffin. OK? Listen…'

'Meteor, stop.'

'Ahhight.'

Eventually she spoke again, shaking her head. 'Sorry… sorry… so…'

He raised his palms.

'They waitin for you.'

'Wot?' His flesh began to crawl.

'They waitin.'

He heard the words in a rush and then again in slow

motion. His eyes narrowed as he cast about into the park's darkness. It was just the usual sights and sounds.

'Wot you sayin?'

She seemed paralysed but as he stepped forward to repeat himself she gripped his arms forcefully.

'She woz gonna cut me, Meteor… put a knife to my eye.'

'Wot? No, no, no, nooooo!' He slipped her grasp and stepped back, placing his hands upon his head. 'You bin settin me up? She get to you?'

She took a step forward, 'Meteor, please.'

He pulled back again sharply as she reached for him, 'Dass why you bin sketchy… an all da phone bizniz!'

'No, no, I woz suppos… it woz Suren who set me up. *She* told dem, den dey all over me. Sayin to bring you to da river tonight. I bin scared dey already watchin. But, I didn' do it, did I?'

He stood before her trembling with rage. She edged closer.

'I bin dead scared, Meteor. You can' say no, you kno. Please… help me.'

A stiletto-point pain bore down into the top of his skull. Fury ripped through him but not towards Jaycee. Predators and prey, same same. His mind teemed with unspeakable havoc.

**IIII**

'You da only one who can save us now, Meteor.'

He was about to snap back when something stopped him. Shock took hold as he considered her words. It was the *us* he couldn't shake. It was true: he'd only been thinking about his own skin. Whatever happened from this moment, Jaycee was as bad as dead. He noticed she'd bitten her lip and blood was showing. Unbidden, another of his mum's cherished sayings floated in: *Never look a gift horse in the mouth, son.* Really? Now. How was he going to save anyone? In real life and not some fantasy. Another voice, like Tru's but not, chipped in: *Best be walkin right now, bruv. Iss on er woteva goes down. Shake da dust. Plenny more fish, innit.*

'God! Fokking hell, bruv!' he shouted at the top of his voice as he turned away. He needed some space. She hadn't followed. He put his face in his hands and tried to think. His fingers smelt of their last meal – all salted fries. The knot in his stomach told him that lingering wasn't an option.

'Meteor?'

When he turned, he could see she was shaking, and before he'd even thought about it, she was in his arms. Yeah. That was that.

# 15

As they ran, he cleared his head best he could. At the park's edge he made Jaycee message A:pex saying she was bringing him to the river as planned. Jaycee's place was near enough to give them time to get to Meteor's before A:pex realised she'd been double-crossed. It was a good plan. Though, how they'd deal with Jaycee's mum was another matter. One step enough.

IIII

The next panicked idea was to catch a bus, but they realised it would likely be quicker on foot. With everything, Jaycee stepped straight out onto the pelican crossing without waiting for the light as a delivery van came thundering past. He yanked at her hoodie desperately enough to clear her head from being clapped by the onrushing wing mirror. She screamed aloud as the horn blared angrily down the road, barely drowning out the barrage of predictable cusses. He dragged her back and sat cradling her curbside to make the shaking stop.

He breathed out heavily. 'I fought you woz a gonna, fo sure.'

'I don kno if I can do this, Meteor.'

He was about to tell her they'd got no choice but, when he opened his mouth, those weren't the words that escaped.

||||

Dodging through the streets as directly as possible took them roughly twenty minutes. The coast was clear when they reached Skye Tower. Annoyingly, the lift was out again but the stairwell looked safe. Blowing, sweaty and a little nauseous, they pushed on up to the thirteenth floor.

Meteor agreed to wait outside the flat – best if Jaycee's mum didn't see him. Anyway, he was glad of the cooldown and rest. He slumped down the opposite wall and checked the time. They still had ten minutes before being expected elsewhere. After a couple of minutes he considered knocking to hurry things along but instead rested an ear against the door. There were raised voices inside.

||||

Five minutes later, Jaycee emerged in tears, her mum close behind. Her hands were not clutching the expected bag.

Mum, a slight but fiery lady, pushed forward to tell Meteor she knew all about boys like him and that she'd call the police or *someone she knew* if he didn't leave straight away. It was made clear he'd never be welcome there and to leave her daughter well alone, oh, and that she knew all about his gang and *where he could be found* if it came to it.

After everything. He was plain lost for words. Her mum continued barking at him as he shifted regard to Jaycee. The warm, endlessly open brown eyes took him back to that first night when they danced together as one, when their bodies so clicked into each other's shape that their hearts had been playing catch up ever since. Before all of this shit. Yet her beauty endured: back then, carefree and flirtatious; now, numb and powerless. Constant. And she hadn't betrayed him when it came to it. At untold cost.

What could he say to her mother right now that would ever help? How would she grasp the threat and danger? How long would it take to convince her, even if she listened? *But you can let them slip through your fingers.* Those were the words of his own mum. Yeah, but, God's own graces were beginning to feel like sand in his hands.

Sudden silence clipped his thoughts. Arms folded, her mum eyed him beadily but no longer seemed intent on blowtorching his soul. He felt dog tired and sick and stressed and... everything else. Do you reach the end because you gave up or do you give up because you've reached the end? He felt there might just be something more he could do. Or maybe he just needed to feel that.

Her mum held out a phone and raised her eyebrows aggressively, even as Jaycee gently held his gaze. He returned it now with his everything. He wouldn't cheapen the moment with words. It'd be goodbye *but only for now*. She'd be safe at least this night. He'd find another way. Maybe even convince the crew. There's always another place, another time.

He turned to face the lonely corridor stretching out ahead. Whilst trudging back toward the stairwell, the door slammed shut behind. He didn't look back but continued on to the sounds of clicking locks. Of all people, Ophelia came to mind! Floating down that unending stream. Well, it was and it wasn't. To the sound of a glorious Gospel choir, she was finally receiving baptism: hands raised in prayer and no longer in desperation, marked forever as the Lord's.

# 16

Halfway down the stairs, the screeching echoes of Jaycee's voice plunged violently down the storeys after him: 'Run, Meteor, run! Dey comin.' Her outline, way above, gestured frantically.

'Sweetheart, I'll be alright. Mum's called da police. Dey'll never get in. Just run! You can still make it.' He hesitated for a moment, considering her words, and then was away at pace. Fifth, fourth, third floor, sec... 'Shit, shit!'

He counted four of them, including *her,* entering the stairwell. One of them, glaring upwards, spotted him. 'Shit, shit!' He turned toe as fast as able, taking as many steps as possible with each leap. The scuffing sounds of frantic pursuit filled his head and he missed his footing a couple of times, skinning his shins.

Floor nine of some twenty. There were bound to be others coming. Needing to be certain, he calculated the risk of crossing to the opposite stairwell in the next corridor up. Opening the fire door, he sprinted hard and then through the far one, leaning out over the guardrails. 'Shit, shit!' Worst fears confirmed: five heading up. Options thinning. He messaged but knew the crew would never get there in time. Only up now. Unless he could give them the slip between floors? Risky – he'd have to let them close distance. Or…

## IIII

Returned to the fateful door, he banged with open palms, shouting louder all the time. Placing his ear to the heavy wood once more revealed the same raised voices. His hammering became increasingly frenetic.

'Jaycee, babes, you gotta let me in. Dey clocked me… gonna kill me, fo real.'

The letterbox flap lifted near his groin. He dropped down to the rectangular parcelling of Jaycee's face. Her lips were wet. 'Oh my God, MUM! They gonna kill im, you gotta open up.'

He could sense the mother's presence nearby. 'I call da po-lice. If dey comin at all, dey comin ta 'elp us, not im.' The flap shut abruptly followed by louder more hysterical shouting.

He had a decision to make. Slamming hammer-fists on the door, he took off in the direction of the second group lower down, hoping to track back into the floor below and behind the first group on the other side. But as he neared the door, a third group came crashing through from God knows where. He skidded to a halt and ran for all he was worth towards the other exit. At just over halfway, the door of his intended escape also opened, and the corridor melted like wax.

# 17

Now he was trapped they took their own sweet time closing in, weapons emerging at leisure here and there. Terror tore through him and he desperately tried Jaycee's door one last time to howls of Wolfpak laughter. The letterbox reopened: 'I can' open it, Meteor. She's got da deadlock key.' Her trembling voice echoed through the corridors of his empty heart as his hands started to shake. This was it, then. Boxed in as usual. Nowhere safe. Never a break.

Despite everything, he felt so grateful it was those consoling lips before his eyes at the very end, and they linked fingers for the briefest eternity.

||||

Fighting the paralysing fear, he raised himself resolutely from the floor. Standing squat and taking in two huge lungfuls of air, he opened out his arms to their fullest extent to touch the walls before shaking them out at the ready. The pulse pounded in his neck as they advanced from both sides. He heard something like his own voice speaking: when you've no choice, that's when you have to choose!

He turned to rush the baseball bat behind rather than face the machete in front, the little difference it made. Lost under a mass of merciless blows, Meteor bled out where he'd fallen to earth.

## IIII

After the laughter and self-congratulation died away, low moans of lamentation and inconsolable weeping filled the corridor. And so, over each of his paling breaths, Jaycee's requiem reached him as though across a great divide. Yet it came to him wrapped within another sound, like the harmonies of a million silver streams. It surged through every note and stay, passing over his mantle, as free as the brightest bird at wing. He could see the park once more and its early sunlight split by the dewfall into a glittering bow of endless colours. And far, and farther still, beyond the high arc of the heavens it flew, beautiful in majesty: the song of the weary soul of the world so happy to be heading home.

# ACKNOWLEDGEMENTS

No story is ever really the work of just one person. Obviously, I'm happy to take all the glory, but there's a silent community of benevolent correction and direction behind each word.

Firstly, thank you to the wonderful people at Troubador Publishing for guidance, support, professionalism and a book! Heartfelt gratitude also goes to the conspicuously talented writer, Kitty Edwards, for some inspirational steers, generosity of spirit and inexhaustible patience (I may have exhausted it). Thanks also to the writer Sam Mills for fine advice that augured a key turning point in my writing journey. Thanks to those willing to suffer earlier drafts – especially lifelong friend, Tom O'Connor, who has walked with me in Word as much as every word; Jonathan and Katie Bryers, without whom I'd be facing the wrong way in the wrong Pimlico townhouse; Claire Gill, who strongly encouraged me to push past the unpublishable; and, Caroline Swanson, who graciously read each draft whilst hating them all, violently. Doffs in abundance to artist Ben East, who matches camaraderie of comedy with literary largesse and priceless portraiture.

With John Donne's celebrated line in mind (no, not the bell, the island), my verbal vanities have been tolerated to varying degrees by my family: Julie, Oliver and Madeleine. Without them, I'd have undoubtedly got a lot more work done. But, perhaps not the right work.

Finally, thanks especially to God for matching me up with the best mentor a writer could ever hope for, Flannery O'Connor.